Padma Shri Pran

Maurice Horn, the editor of World Encyclopedia of Comics, has described cartoonist PRAN as Walt Disney of India.

Entertaining generation after generation, his comics have been constant companion of all the growing youngsters providing fun and amusement through his famous characters like CHACHA CHAUDHARY, SABU, SHRIMATIJI, PINKI, BILLOO, RAMAN etc. More than 600 of his titles are selling well in the market, and numerous comic strips are regularly appearing in various newspapers. His CHACHA CHAUDHARY comics had already been adapted for a TV Serial, and ran continuously for 600 episodes on a premier channel.

Travelling widely over the globe, he delivers lectures at various International Conferences. He has also been honoured with 'People of The Year Award' by Limca Book of Records for popularizing comics. His comic book 'United We Stand' was released in 1983 by the then Prime Minister Mrs. Indira Gandhi, and is still very popular among children.

Publisher

ANYWAY, TAKE THESE, AND TRY!
NOW SAY- WHO IS TALLER?
HA ! HA !!
THEN HOW CAN MY HEIGHT BE INCREASED?
SIMPLE! WITH DRINKING MILK!
GULP-GULP-P-P !

I HAVE CONSUMED MILK! STILL HEIGHT IS NOT INCREASED!
I MEANT MILK MAKES BONES STRONGER. AS YOU GROW, YOU'LL GAIN HEIGHT!
DADAJI! HOW CAN BE I TALLER?
STAND ON STOOL! YOU'LL BECOME TALLER!
IF YOU WANT TO BE MORE TALLER, THEN CLIMB ON LADDER!
DADU CUTS JOKES OF EVERYTHING!
WWW.CHACHACHAUDHARY.COM
© PRAN'S FEATURES

BHIKU! I WANT TO INCREASE MY HEIGHT!
PINKI! WHY DO YOU WANT TO BUY TROUBLE?
IT IS BENEFICIAL TO BE SMALL! IF YOU BECOME TALL, YOU'LL NEED MORE CLOTH FOR YOUR FROCK! YOU'LL NEED MORE FOOD TO EAT!
IN HIGHER CLASSES, YOU'LL HAVE TO STUDY THICK BOOKS!
PEOPLE CONSIDER YOU GENIUS, WHEREAS YOUR BRAIN CONTAINS FODDER!
DON'T BE ANGRY! AN IDEA JUST STRUCK ME!

MUMMY! COME AND SEE!
MUMMY !
OMPH! THIS GIRL DON'T LET ME WORK!
MUMMY--MUMMY--
NOW SAY, WHO IS TALLER?
??
OHH !
I HAD SUSPICION OF SOMETHING WRONG!

A PUZZLE

NANI! WHICH BOOK ARE YOU READING?
INTERESTING PUZZLES !
ARE THOSE EXCITING ?
YES! AND KNOWLEDGEABLE TOO!
WWW.CHACHACHAUDHARY.COM
© PRAN'S FEATURES

DURING CHILDHOOD WE FRIENDS ASK EACH OTHER QUIZZES!
WE ENJOYED A LOT!
NOW CHILDREN ARE IN SO HURRY, THEY HAVE NO TIME FOR THESE!
OKAY! ASK ME A QUIZ!
ANSWER--TWO HENS AHEAD OF A HEN, TWO HENS BEHIND A HEN!

HOW MANY TOTAL HENS ARE THERE ?
THINK BEFORE ANSWER!
THREE IN ALL!
HOW ?
TWO HENS BEHIND FIRST HEN----
TWO HENS AHEAD OF THIRD ONE HEN! TOTAL THREE!

YOU ARE SMART!
THANKS!
NOW, CAN I ASK YOU ONE QUIZ?
I AM READY!
THREE FEMALES WERE SITTING ON A BENCH!
ONE HAD A CHILD ON HER LAP! SECOND HAD A MANGAL SUTRA AROUND HER NECK!

THIRD ONE HAD A WEDDING RING ON HER FINGER! AMONG THE THREE, ONE WAS NOT MARRIED! SAY WHICH ONE?
ONE HAD A RING ON HER FINGER, SECOND HAD MANGAL SUTRA! THIRD ONE HAD A CHILD ON HER LAP ?-- SORRY, I AM PUZZLED!
A QUIZ IS USUALLY PUZZLING!
SORRY! I HAVE NO ANSWER!
ONE WHO HAD A CHILD! THAT CHILD WAS HER YOUNGER BROTHER!
SHE WAS SIXTEEN YEARS OLD!
HA! HA! VERY GOOD!
NANI! BYE!

DICTIONARY
STUDENTS! I AM GIVING YOU FIVE SANSKRIT WORDS FOR HOMEWORK!
YOU'LL HAVE TO TRANSLATE THOSE TO ENGLISH!
WORDS ARE- 1. SUSWADUTOYA, 2. PISHUNASYA, 3. TADAGA, 4. BHAGINI, 5. JALKUPI!
© PRAN'S FEATURES

I'LL DO HOMEWORK FIRST, WHEN I REACH THERE!
I HAVE COMPLETED ENGLISH, MATHS, AND HINDI! ONLY SANSKRIT IS LEFT!
OHH! I CAN'T DO SANSKRIT'S TRANSLATION TO ENGLISH!
WHO CAN GUIDE ME ?
MOM! CAN YOU HELP ME IN SANSKRIT?
SORRY, BABY! I HAD NOT STUDIED SANSKRIT SUBJECT!
OUR NEIGHBOUR JHAPATJI IS A WISE MAN! HE CAN HELP YOU!

UNCLE! COULD YOU HELP ME IN DOING TRANSLATION OF SANSKRIT ?
SORRY! I DO NOT HAVE SANSKRIT DICTIONARY!
YOU OFTEN BOAST TO BE A BALMIKI AND GIVE KNOWLEDGE TO OTHERS!
CAN'T HELP A CHILD ?
MY FRIEND BHIKU IS INTELLIGENT! HE CAN HELP!
BUT HIS HOUSE IS FAR OFF!

YOU CAN USE MY MOBILE PHONE!
BHIKU! DO YOU POSSESS SANSKRIT-ENGLISH DICTIONARY?
NO!
THEN YOU MIGHT NOT HAVE DONE THE HOMEWORK?
I HAVE TRANSLATED SANSKRIT WORDS!
YOU CAN WRITE ANSWER-
1. SUSWADUTOYA - TASTY WATER!

2. PISHUNASYA-BACK BITING!
3. TADAGA- POND!
4. BHAGINI- SISTER!
5. JALKUPI - A BOTTLE OF WATER!
ASK HIM, HOW COULD HE ANSWER WITHOUT A DICTIONARY?
BHIKU! HOW COULD YOU FIND ANSWERS ?
I HAVE A SOFTWARE OF SANSKRIT-ENGLISH DICTIONARY IN MY COMPUTER!
THAT HELPED ME IN TRANSLATION!
NOW CHILDREN DO NOT REMAIN KIDS!
WWW.CHACHACHAUDHARY.COM

PINKI, THE PAINTER
DADAJI! A PAINTER UNCLE HAS GIFTED ME TWO BRUSHES!
WOW!
WHAT SHOULD I DO WITH THESE ?
PAINT SOME GOOD PICTURES WITH THESE!
A GOOD IDEA!
© PRAN'S FEATURES

I'LL DRAW A BEAUTIFUL PICTURE!
IF BUSY, SHE'LL NOT BE MISCHIEVOUS.
I ALREADY HAVE A CANVAS AND COLOURS!
LET ME START WORKING!
I'LL MAKE PAINTING MY HOBBY!
HERE I'LL BEGIN!

DADAJI! WHERE IS PINKI ?
SHE IS BUSY IN HER ROOM!
SHE MAY NOT BE ABLE TO MEET ANYONE!

BUT THIS IS OUR PLAYING TIME!
SHE CAN'T! SHE IS BUSY IN PAINTING!
PINKI,-- A PAINTER ?
LET ME SEE, WHAT IS SHE DRAWING ?
OBSTINATE CHILD!

NATTU! HOW DO YOU LIKE MY PICTURE ?
MY MOUTH WATERS TO LOOK AT THAT!
I HAVE PAINTED ARTISTIC DESIGN! HOW DOES YOUR MOUTH WATER TO SEE IT?
I THOUGHT YOU'VE PAINTED JALEBIS! (A SWEET)
WWW.CHACHACHAUDHARY.COM

LAZY
LET ME DOWNLOAD THIS CARTOON MOVIE!
WWW.CHACHACHAUDHARY.COM
MOM! I WANT WATER!
© PRAN'S FEATURES

BABY! I AM NOT FREE!
I AM BUSY IN WASHING CLOTHES!
YOU CAN TAKE WATER FROM KITCHEN!
I DON'T WANT TO LEAVE COMPUTER!

FIFTEEN MINUTES LATER--
MOM! GIVE ME WATER!
LET ME DO MY WORK!
DON'T BE LAZY!
GET UP, GO AND DRINK WATER!

MOM--WATER--
NOW IF YOU DISTURB ME AGAIN, I'LL COME TO SLAP YOU HARD!
IF YOU COME TO SLAP, BRING WATER ALONG!
I CAN'T WIN YOU!
HERE IS WATER! YOU HAVE BECOME VERY LAZY!

IN ADJOINING ROOM..
NEWS CHANNEL TELECASTS LIVE NATIONAL AND INTERNATIONAL EVENTS!
TV
DAUGHTER-IN- LAW! GIVE ME A GLASS OF WATER!
I CAN'T LEAVE TV!
MOM! EVERYBODY IS LAZY IN THIS HOUSE!

FATTY
WOW! WHAT AN INTERESTING COMEDY?
HA! HA!
I AM ENJOYING THIS CARTOON MOVIE!
© PRAN'S FEATURES
WWW.CHACHACHAUDHARY.COM

GOOD MOVIE AND POTATO CHIPS! DOUBLE ENJOYMENT!
DING ! DONG !!
WHO HAS COME TO DISTURB ?
LET ME SEE!
FATTY! YOU?

COME, LET US GO TO PLAY.
SORRY! I AM WATCHING CARTOON MOVIE!
THEN I'LL TOO SEE THAT!
THERE IS ONLY ONE SOFA!
AND I HAVE OCCUPIED IT!
WHERE WOULD YOU SIT ?

I'LL SIT ON YOUR LAP!
NOW WE BOTH CAN SEE TV!
GET UP! YOU HAVE LOADED ME!
YOUR WEIGHT IS HEAVY! I CAN'T BEAR IT!
IN FRIENDSHIP, ONE HAS TO MAKE ADJUSTMENT!

I AM HUNGRY!
YOU CAN TAKE MY CHIPS! BUT GET UP!
ENJOY MOVIE! I'LL STAND UP DURING ADVERTISEMENTS!
I AM HIDDEN DUE TO YOUR FIGURE!
I CAN'T SEE TV! HOW CAN I ENJOY MOVIE?
WHEN I LAUGH, YOU TOO LAUGH!

MONEY FOR CHOCOLATE
PINKI! WHERE ARE YOU GOING ?
TO NANI'S HOUSE, TO EAT CHOCOLATES?
WWW.CHACHACHAUDHARY.COM
DOES YOUR NANI HAVE A LOT OF CHOCOLATES ?
NO! I'LL TAKE MONEY FROM HER TO BUY ONE!
NANI! I WANT TO EAT CHOCOLATE!
© PRAN'S FEATURES
YOU COME TO ME, WHEN YOU WISH TO EAT THAT!

MY RIGHT HAND HOLDS A TEN RUPEES NOTE, AND LEFT HAND HOLDS A HUNDRED RUPEES NOTE ! YOU CAN TAKE ANY ONE OF TWO TO BUY CHOCOLATE !
I'LL TAKE TEN RUPEES NOTE!
L STORES
GIVE ME ONE CHOCOLATE!
PINKI! I OFFERED YOU A HUNDRED RUPEES NOTE TOO! WHY DID NOT YOU PICK THAT?
I KNEW, THE DAY I PICK A HUNDRED RUPEES NOTE, YOU'LL NOT GIVE ME MONEY IN FUTURE!

PINKI
MOBILE AND GOAT
ALI HAD A GOAT, WHO WAS VERY NAUGHTY---
HOW DOES A GOAT LOOK LIKE ? I'VE NEVER SEEN IT BEFORE.
© PRAN'S FEATURES
I'LL ASK DIDI ABOUT IT.
YES, PRIYA ! APPLY THE RULE OF DEMAND AND SUPPLY.

DIDI !
IT APPLIES ON AGRICULTURAL AND INDUSTRIAL GOODS AS WELL.
DON'T KNOW WHEN WILL THEIR TALKS END ?
AFTER HALF HOUR---
I WANT TO ASK YOU SOMETHING ?
OOMPH !
WHAT ANIMAL IS A GOAT ?
IT'S AN ANIMAL LARGER THAN A CAT BUT SMALLER THAN A HORSE.
I'LL BRING IT.
SORRY PRIYA ! I'VE TO CUT THE CALL-

DIDI ! I'VE BROUGHT A GOAT.
LOOK !
WHAT ?
THAT'S A DOG. GO AND LEAVE HIM FROM WHERE YOU HAVE BROUGHT HIM.
OK ! DIDI.

HELLO, RICHA MOTWANI ! HOW IS YOUR STUDY GOING ON ?ARE YOU WATCHING THE FASHION SHOW ON TV ?
DIDI !
YES, THAT IS A GOAT.
HIS NAME IS BAASHA. I BORROWED HIM FROM BASHIR MIAN.
I'LL FETCH SOMETHING TO EAT FOR HIM.
HERE, EAT CHAPATIS.

PHONE BASHIR MIAN. HE SHOULD COME AND SEE HOW IS HIS ANIMAL HAPPY ?
HE WAS HUNGRY !
YES !
OHH ! WHERE IS MY MOBILE PHONE ?
I MIGHT HAVE FORGOTTEN IT IN THE KITCHEN.
IT IS NOT HERE.
TRY DIALING YOUR PHONE FROM OTHER NUMBER. YOU'LL LOCATE IT WHEN IT'S BELL RINGS.

IT IS GOOD IDEA.
I'LL DIAL THE NUMBER.
THE BELL IS RINGING.
??
WHEN YOU PLACED CHAPATIS BEFORE HIM, YOU MIGHT HAVE DROPPED YOUR PHONE WHICH THE ANIMAL SWALLOWED.

PINKI
GRANDPA'S PURSE
GRANDPA ! WHY ARE YOU GETTING READY ?
I'VE TO GO TO OFFICE.
YOU SAID, YOU GOT RETIRED ?
YES ! CAN'T I GO THERE TO TAKE MY PENSION ?
THEN TO WHY GO THERE SO SMARTINGLY ?
I WAS A HIGH OFFICER THERE.

WERE YOU AS HIGH AS THE ROOF ?
NO, STUPID ! THAT MEANS I WAS HOLDING A BIG POST, LIKE-A SUPERINTENDENT.
?
WHY ARE YOU RUNNING BACK ?
I FORGOT MY PURSE THERE.
OHH ! MY PURSE ?
WHAT HAPPENED ?
I PLACED MY PURSE HERE. IT HAS VANISHED.

BUT YOU'LL GET PENSION FROM OFFICE.
DO I NEED MONEY FOR BUS FARE OR NOT ?
THERE IS MY PURSE IN THE MOUTH OF KUTKUT.
THROW THE PURSE OR I'LL HIT YOU.
CRACK!
OHH !

OOWW ! MY FANCY LIGHT.
WHERE IS THAT SQUIRREL ?
THERE SHE IS.
PUT IT DOWN !
I'LL SWITCH ON THE FAN !
NO ! KUTKUT WILL DIE.

JUMPP !
OOHH !
??
THANKS ! SHE DROPPED MY PURSE FROM HER MOUTH.
BUT WHERE IS MY FIVE HUNDRED RUPEE NOTE WHICH I HAD KEPT IN IT ?
KUTKUT IS HOLDING IT IN HER MOUTH .
PUT THAT ON GROUND.
GIVE THAT TO ME.

GRRRRR!
MY NOTE.
GRANDPA ! RUN FAST OR YOU'LL MISS THE BUS.

LET US LEARN YOGA

Available in Hindi , English, Marathi, Gujarati,Bangla & Odia

Today the whole world is inclined towards Yoga. This is the high time when we can promote Yoga to our children and inculcate its benefits in to them. We have to make them understand about its importance, so that they could become hale & healthy, mentally & physically both.

This book is going to update our children about Yoga, and it would be very easy for them to understand the method of doing each asana.

In this way, they not only will enjoy Yoga, but also going to develop concentration, which in turn help them to achieve big."

Diamond BOOKS
X-30, Okhla Industrial Area Phase-II, New Delhi-110020, Ph.: +91-011-40712200
Email: sales@dpb.in, website:www.diamondbook.in

Help every duckling to find its own way to the little pond in the middle of the maze.

Discover Talent @ Diamond Toons
X-30, Okhla Industrial Area, Phase-II, New Delhi-110020
Ph.: 011-40712100, 40712200, E-mail: sales@dpb.in

Diamond TOONS
चाचा चौधरी और प्रोफेसर बैड
बिल्लू और नारियल का पेड़
पिंकी मूछड़ सिंह
छोटा भीम उड़ने वाला कालीन
बिल्लू की गर्लफ्रेंड
पिंकी फन-डे
चाचा चौधरी, बिल्लू और पिंकी कॉमिक्स अब डाइजेस्ट में भी उपलब्ध।
चाचा चौधरी डाइजेस्ट-1
चाचा चौधरी डाइजेस्ट-2
चाचा चौधरी डाइजेस्ट-3
चाचा चौधरी डाइजेस्ट-4
पिंकी डाइजेस्ट-2
अपने चर्चित पात्रों चाचा चौधरी, साबू बिल्लू और पिंकी के माध्यम से ट्रेन यात्रा के दौरान एवं गर्मी की छुट्टियों के बीच हमें हंसाने और प्रेरित करने वाले लोकप्रिय पात्र।
X-30, ओखला इंडस्ट्रियल एरिया, फेज-2, नई दिल्ली-110020 फोन न.: 011-40712100, 40712200, ई-मेल : sales@dpb.in

The Great Indian Biography Series

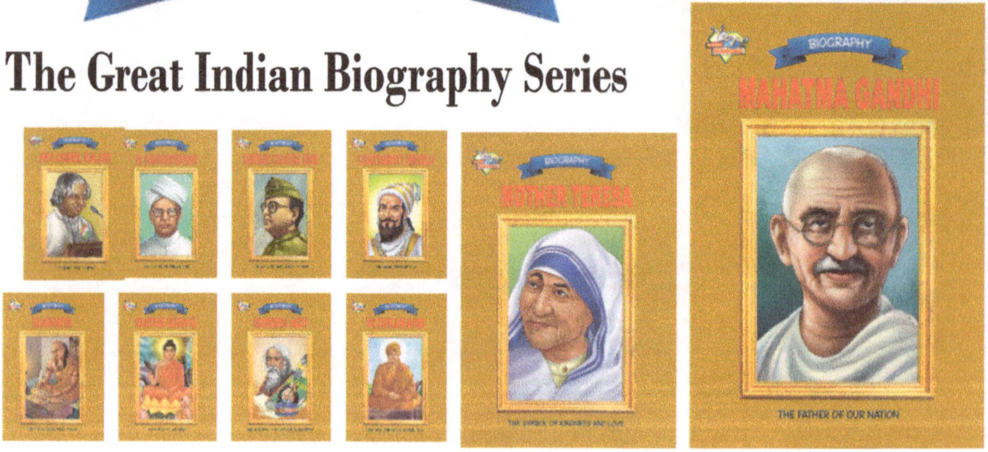

Available in Hindi & English

Order Now

X-30, Okhla Industrial Area Phase-II, New Delhi-110020, INDIA
Tel.: 40716600 E-mail: sales@dpb.in, Website: www.dpb.in